MOONBEAM
FINDS
A MOON STONE

SELMA AND JACK
WASSERMANN

ILLUSTRATIONS
GEORGE ROHRER

BENEFIC PRESS · CHICAGO

The Moonbeam Books

MOONBEAM IS CAUGHT

MOONBEAM AT THE ROCKET PORT

MOONBEAM AND THE ROCKET RIDE

MOONBEAM AND DAN STARR

MOONBEAM FINDS A MOON STONE

MOONBEAM AND SUNNY

Library of Congress
Number 66-12804

Copyright 1967 by Benefic Press
All Rights Reserved
Printed in the United States of America

CONTENTS

The Big Rocket

"Stop jumping, Moonbeam!" said Dr. Jim.

Moonbeam, the little space chimp, did not stop. She jumped up and down.

"Do you want to go up in the big rocket tomorrow?" said Dr. Jim . "Then you must stop jumping. I must have a good look at you."

Up and down jumped Moonbeam.

Scott looked at the little chimp and laughed. He worked with Moonbeam, and he was her friend. Now he was helping Dr. Jim with little Moonbeam. But Moonbeam did not help.

"Moonbeam must have moon fever," said Scott. "She cannot wait for tomorrow. She wants to take off for the moon right now!"

"Hoon! Hoon!" said Moonbeam. Then she jumped up on Dr. Jim.

"Now I cannot look at you at all, little chimp!" said Dr. Jim. "What are we going to do with this chimp?" he said to Scott.

Scott looked at Dr. Jim and Moonbeam. He smiled at them.

"This is the day for the big moon rocket to come out," Scott said. "Moonbeam could go to see it. It may stop her moon fever."

"It could work," said Dr. Jim. "Then she would stop all this jumping and running around. Will you go with her to see the rocket she will ride in, Scott?"

Scott looked at the time.

"I cannot go away from here now," he said. "I have work to do."

"I will go with her then," said Dr. Jim. "Come on, Moonbeam."

"Hoon! Hoon!" said Moonbeam.

"See you soon, Moonbeam!" said Scott.

Moonbeam went out with Dr. Jim.

"Here is my jeep," Dr. Jim said. "Jump in!"
Moonbeam jumped into the jeep with Dr. Jim,
and away they went.

On and on went the jeep. Moonbeam and Dr.
Jim saw no one on the road. They saw no other
car at all.

Then Moonbeam did see something.

"Heen, hon, hon, hoon! Hoon!" she said.

"I see it, too, Moonbeam," said Dr. Jim.
"That is where the big rockets are made."

Dr. Jim made the jeep slow down. Then he
stopped it.

"Here we are," he said. "We can look on
from here."

Moonbeam jumped out. Dr. Jim came, too. Then Dr. Jim stopped and looked up.

"Look, Moonbeam!" he said. "Here it comes! Here comes the rocket!"

Big doors opened. Moonbeam looked in. She saw the big moon rocket. Then, little by little, the big rocket came out. Men came out with the big rocket. They worked on it.

The rocket moved very slowly. It was very, very big. It was so big that it made the men look very little.

"This is YOUR rocket, Moonbeam," said Dr.
Jim. "Tomorrow you will go up in it. You will
ride right up to the moon!"

"Hoon! Hoon!" said Moonbeam.

But she did not want to wait for tomorrow.
She wanted to go now. So Moonbeam ran away
from Dr. Jim. She ran up to the moon rocket
and jumped for it. Up and up she went.

"Come back here!" called Dr. Jim. "This is
not the time for the moon trip."

Up and up and up
went little Moonbeam.

"Come down here!"
called Dr. Jim. "Come
on down, Moonbeam!"

But Moonbeam did
not come down. She
had moon fever. She
wanted to go up to the
moon right away.

Then a working man
saw Moonbeam. But
she did not see him.
He went after her—
and soon he had her.
Down he came with her.

10

"Good work!" said Dr. Jim.

But Moonbeam did not like it. She looked down. Dr. Jim laughed.

"Come on, Moonbeam," he said. "Let's go back now. Tomorrow will come soon."

He put Moonbeam into the jeep and jumped in. Soon the jeep was on its way.

Trouble for Dr. Jim

The jeep went on.

Moonbeam liked jeep rides. She liked to look out. But now Moonbeam did not look out. She was not happy.

"Heen! Hon, hon," she said.

Dr. Jim laughed. He looked at Moonbeam. "What are we going to do with you?" he said.

"Heen!" said Moonbeam.

"You will soon be on your way to the moon," said Dr. Jim. "You must stop this moon fever."

Moonbeam looked up. She saw something on the road, right where the jeep was going. Dr. Jim was looking at Moonbeam. He did not see what was on the road.

"Heeeeeeen! Heeeeeeeeeen!" said Moonbeam.

Dr. Jim looked. He had to stop the jeep fast. Off the road went the jeep.

"Look out!" said Dr. Jim.

A very big stone was in the jeep's way. When the jeep hit the stone, it stopped too fast. Dr. Jim hit his head on the jeep.

Moonbeam looked at Dr. Jim. He did not look back at her.

"Hoon, hon, hon, heen," said Moonbeam.

Dr. Jim did not laugh. He did not look at Moonbeam. He did not move. Moonbeam went to him. She tried to get his head up. It did not help. Dr. Jim was hurt.

"Heeeeeen! Heeeeen!" said Moonbeam.

She jumped out of the jeep. She had no moon fever now. She had to find help for Dr. Jim.

But where could help come from?

Moonbeam looked up and down the road. No cars were coming. She saw no people.

Then Moonbeam did see something. It was a lookout tower not far from the road and the jeep. Will a man be up in the tower?

Moonbeam ran to the tower. Then she made her way up the tower. Up and up she went. Soon she was all the way up. And she did find a man up there!

"A chimp!" said the lookout man. "What are you doing here?"

"Hon, hon, hon, hon," said Moonbeam.

She wanted help for Dr. Jim. But the man could not know that she wanted help.

"What is it, little chimp?" he said.

"Hon, hon," said Moonbeam. "Hon, hon, heen, hon hon!"

The man in the lookout tower looked and looked at little Moonbeam.

"Do you want to play?" he said. He went after her.

Moonbeam liked to play. But this was no time for play. Dr. Jim must have help.

"Heeeeen! Heeeeen!" she said.

She jumped away from the man. And she ran down the tower. The man looked after her as she ran.

"Stop!" he called. "Come back!"

But Moonbeam did not go back. She went on. Soon she was back on the road.

A car was coming. Moonbeam saw it. She jumped up and down in the road.

"Hoon! Hon, hon, hon," she said.

When the man in the car saw Moonbeam, he stopped. And Moonbeam jumped right in!

"A chimp? Here?" said the man.

"Hon, hon, heen, hon, hon," said Moonbeam.

The man was very friendly. But he, too, did not know that Moonbeam wanted help.

"I will go into town with this little chimp," he said. "There they will know what to do with her."

The car went on. It came to where the jeep was stopped.

"Heen, hon, hon, hoon!" said Moonbeam.

But the man did not know what Moonbeam wanted. And he did not see Dr. Jim in the jeep. So he did not stop his car!

"Heen! Heeeeeeeen!" said Moonbeam.

"You are a funny chimp!" said the man.

Moonbeam wanted to get out of the car. But the car was going too fast. And she did not see a way out.

On and on went the car. It came into town. Soon the car had to stop for a light.

"See that man, little chimp?" said the man in the car. "He will know what to do with you. We will go to him."

But Moonbeam did not see. She did not hear what the man in the car said. She was working on a way to get out of the car. Soon she found the way, and out she jumped!

"Stop!" called the man in the car. "Stop that chimp! Stop her!"

But Moonbeam did not stop.

Moonbeam and the Twins

Moonbeam ran away from the car. The people in the town saw her run.

"Stop that chimp!" they called out.

They ran after her. But chimps are fast. Moonbeam jumped this way and that. She ran as fast as a chimp can run. The people in town could not catch her.

People came out of their houses to see what was going on. Cars stopped, and the people in them came out.

"Stop that chimp!" they all called.

And they all ran after her.

But the people could not catch Moonbeam. She ran too fast. Soon she was so far away from them, they could not tell what way she went. But Moonbeam ran on and on.

She ran out of town. She ran and ran and
ran. Then she had to slow down. And then
she stopped. She looked one way, and then she
looked the other way. Where to, now?

Moonbeam did not know what to do. She
wanted to find Scott. Scott would know how
to help Dr. Jim. But Moonbeam did not know
where to look for Scott.

"Heeeeen," she said.

"What was that?" said two voices.

Moonbeam looked up. Two girls were coming. And one girl was just like the other!

When the girls saw Moonbeam, they stopped.

"Look, Jenny!" said one girl.

"It's a chimp, Penny!" said the other girl.

"What is a chimp doing here?" said Penny.

"I don't know," said Jenny. "But we can play with it. And then we can take it home with us!"

But Moonbeam did not want to play now. She wanted to find Scott.

"Heen! Heen!" she said.

"What is it, little chimp?" said Penny.

"Hon, hon, heen, hon, hon!" said Moonbeam.

"What is the trouble, little chimp?" said Jenny. "We will help you."

"Heeeeen! Hon, hon, hon," said Moonbeam.

The girls could not tell what the trouble was. They tried to play with Moonbeam. But she backed away from them.

Then Penny looked up. Far off she saw the towers of the Rocket Port.

"I know, Jenny!" she said. "See the rocket towers? This little chimp must be from the Rocket Port!"

"Hoon! Hoon!" said Moonbeam.

"You must be right!" said Jenny. "This must be a space chimp!"

"Come on, little chimp!" said Penny. "We will have you back at the Rocket Port in no time at all!"

24

"Hoon! Hoon!" said Moonbeam.

Moonbeam went with the two girls. They did not have far to go. Then the girls stopped.

"Look, little chimp!" said Jenny. "There is the gate to the Rocket Port."

When Moonbeam saw the gate, she ran to it.

"Wait, little chimp!" called Penny.

"We want to come with you!" called Jenny. Moonbeam did not wait for the girls.

"Stop!" said the man at the gate.

Moonbeam did not stop for the man at the gate. She ran right by him into the Rocket Port. On and on she ran. Men tried to stop her, but they could not catch her.

Then a voice called, "Moonbeam!" The chimp stopped. It was Scott's voice.

Where Is Dr. Jim?

When Moonbeam saw Scott, she ran to him.

"Hoon! Hoon! Hon, hon, heen!" she said, and jumped on him.

Scott laughed. Then he stopped laughing.

"Where is Dr. Jim?" he asked.

"Heeeeen! Heeeeen!" said Moonbeam.

"Dr. Jim must be in trouble," said Scott. Then he asked Moonbeam, "Can you help me to find him?"

"Hon, hon, hon, hon," said Moonbeam.

"Come on, then!" said Scott.

Scott and Moonbeam jumped into Scott's jeep, and off they went.

"Where did you come from?" Scott asked Moonbeam. "How did you get back here? Where is Dr. Jim?"

"Heen! Hon, hon, hon," said Moonbeam.

"And where do we go now?" asked Scott.

"Hon, hon, heen, hon, hon," said Moonbeam.

"That is no help at all," said Scott.

By that time, the jeep was at the gate. The man at the gate looked at Moonbeam.

"Stop!" he called out. "That's the one! This is the chimp that ran by me!"

Scott stopped the jeep.

"You saw Moonbeam come?" he asked the man. "How did she get here?"

"It was the girls," said the man at the gate. "The girls came with her. Now they are on their way home."

"The girls?" said Scott. "What girls? There are no girls here."

"Look!" said the man. "You can still see them. There, down the road."

Scott looked down the road. The girls were far away by now. Scott could just see them.

"Come on!" he said to Moonbeam. "We must catch up with them. They will tell us where they found you."

Scott and Moonbeam jumped back into the jeep. The jeep went fast. Then Scott called, "Girls! Stop!"

The girls stopped and looked at the jeep.

"It's that chimp again!" they said.

"It was good of you girls to help Moonbeam," said Scott. "Now you can help me, too. Where did you find Moonbeam?"

"It was not far from town," said Penny.

"We can help you find it," said Jenny.

"Get in, then!" said Scott.

Again the jeep went fast. The girls looked out as they rode in the jeep.

"Go this way now!" Jenny said.

Scott went that way. Then Penny called out, "Now go there!"

Scott turned there. Soon the girls said, "This is it. Here is where we found Moonbeam."

"Hoon! Hon, hon," said Moonbeam.

"Hmmmm," said Scott. He looked around. "I don't see Dr. Jim's jeep," he said.

"Heen! Heen!" said Moonbeam.

"How did you get here, Moonbeam?" asked Scott as he turned to Moonbeam.

"Look!" said the girls.

A car was coming down the road. Three men were in it. When the men saw Moonbeam, the car came to a stop.

"So there you are, chimp!" said a voice from the car. "We were looking for you."

Moonbeam looked in the back of the car. She saw the man who had picked her up on the road not far from Dr. Jim's jeep!

"Why were you looking for Moonbeam?" Scott wanted to know.

"I found this chimp on the road," said the man. "But she ran away from me."

"Where did you find her?" asked Scott. "We must get there fast."

"I will go with you," said the man. "Then you will see."

Scott, Moonbeam, the two girls, and the three men from the car all jumped into the jeep. Off went the jeep. It was not a long ride. But with all the people together in one jeep, it was a funny ride.

Then the man called out, "This is it! This is where I picked her up!" Scott stopped the jeep. He looked around.

"It's that chimp again!" came a voice from far away. It was the man in the lookout tower. He came running down from the tower.

"So he saw Moonbeam, too," said Scott.

When the lookout man came, Scott asked him, "Was there a man with Moonbeam?"

"No," said the lookout man. "I did not see a man with the chimp."

Then one of the girls saw something down the road.

"Look!" she said.

"It's a jeep!" said one of the men.

"Good work, Penny!" said Scott. "Come on!"

Scott jumped into his jeep. Moonbeam ran. The two girls and the other men ran after Moonbeam and the jeep.

Then Scott stopped his jeep. He ran to Dr.
Jim's jeep. The others came, too.

"There he is!" said Scott. He looked at Dr.
Jim. "He is hurt, but he will be all right after
a little time."

"Hoon! Hoon!" said Moonbeam.

The men helped Scott with Dr. Jim. Slowly
they picked him up.

"Look out for his head!" said Scott. "I think
it is hurt."

They put Dr. Jim in Scott's jeep.

"You go on," said one of the men. "Get him back to the Rocket Port. We will stay here and look after his jeep."

Soon Scott's jeep was on its way back to the Rocket Port. In it were Scott, Moonbeam, and Dr. Jim.

"That was good work, Moonbeam!" said Scott. "With your good help, we found Dr. Jim in time. Now he will be all right."

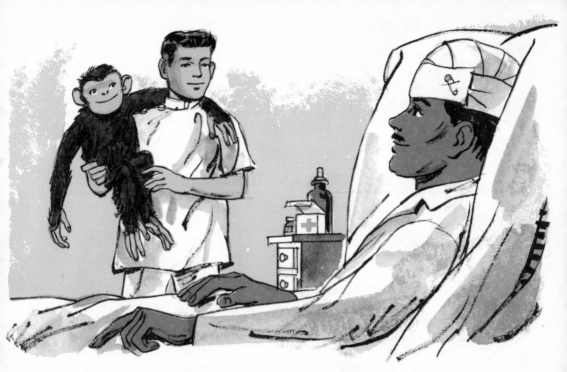

A Piece of the Moon

The day of the moon trip came.

"Come, Moonbeam," said Scott. "We will go to see Dr. Jim. Then it will be time for the rocket to lift off for the moon."

"Hoon! Hoon!" said Moonbeam. But when she saw Dr. Jim, she said, "Heeeeeeeen!"

Dr. Jim laughed. "Do I look so funny to you, Moonbeam?" he said.

Moonbeam looked at Dr. Jim. The hurt part of his head was all in white. It did not look good. But Dr. Jim laughed again.

"This will soon come off," he said. "I will be all right."

Then Dr. Jim looked at Scott.

"How is it going, Scott?" he asked.

"Will Moonbeam be off on her trip soon?"

"Very soon," said Scott. "From here we will go to put Moonbeam's space suit on. Then —off to the rocket."

The two men were not looking at Moonbeam. They did not see how she was playing. When it was time to go, Scott looked around.

"I don't see the chimp in here," he said. "Where did she go?"

"She did not go out," said Dr. Jim. "We would have seen her go. She must be right around here. Let's look for her."

The two men looked around them. Then they saw something white. It looked like a white chimp! The white chimp tried to move.

"Heen! Heen, heen, heen!" it said.

The two men laughed and laughed. Little by little, Moonbeam came out.

"Moonbeam saw that my head was all in white," said Dr. Jim. "She wanted to be in white, too."

Then Scott looked at little Moonbeam.

"Be happy that you do not have a hurt head, Moonbeam," he said to her.

Scott looked at the time. "We will have to go now," he said.

"Have a good trip, Moonbeam," said Dr. Jim. "And pick up a piece of the moon for me!"

Moonbeam went out with Scott.

Now Moonbeam did not have long to wait. Soon she had her space suit on.

"Did you hear what Dr. Jim said?" asked Scott. "He wants a piece of the moon! Will you find one for him?"

"Hoon! Hoon!" said little Moonbeam.

Three men came in. "Look, Moonbeam!" said Scott. "Here are the astronauts. You will ride to the moon with them."

Moonbeam looked at the astronauts. She saw her friend, Dan Starr. He was the head astronaut for this trip. Moonbeam did not know the other two men.

"Here you are, Moonbeam," Dan Starr's voice came out of his space suit. "Are you happy you are going on this big space ride?"

"Hoon! Hoon!" came Moonbeam's voice.

"Good!" said Dan. "It's time to go."

Scott and Moonbeam went in one jeep. The astronauts went in the other jeep. The jeeps went fast, and then—there was the big rocket!

Men were all around the rocket. Some were working on it. Others were just looking. They were waiting to see Moonbeam and the three astronauts lift off.

"There are the men!" they said. "There is the chimp!"

"Have a good trip, Moonbeam!" said one of the men.

"Have a good ride!" said others.

Slowly, Scott, Moonbeam, and the astronauts made their way. Then a voice said:

"Astronauts and chimp—into the rocket! All others—wait at the rocket gate!"

Moonbeam and the astronauts went on to the rocket. Scott came with Moonbeam.

All around them, men worked fast.

Then the astronauts came to the rocket. Up and in they went. Scott and Moonbeam came right after them. Scott helped Moonbeam into the rocket ship.

Then Scott said, "It's time for me to get back now, Moonbeam. This rocket soon will go up. Have a good time on the moon!"

Moonbeam looked at Scott.

"Hon, hon, hon, hon," she said.

"See you when you get back!" said Scott to Dan Starr and the other astronauts.

Dan laughed.

"Don't wait up for us!" he said.

Then Scott went out. He came away from the rocket and back to the gate. The working men stopped working on the rocket and came away from it.

All was still. The people at the gate all looked and waited. Scott waited with them. In the rocket, three astronauts and little Moonbeam waited.

Then came that voice,

". . .THREE. . ."

All the people looked at the big rocket.

". . .TWO. . ."

The rocket waited.

". . .ONE. . ."

No other voice was heard. All was still.

". . .LIFT OFF!. . ."

"Ahhhhh!" said the people. It looked like a big light was going on under the rocket. Slowly, the big rocket pushed up from the Rocket Port. For a time, it looked as if it would come to a stop again. Then, little by little, the rocket went faster.

Scott looked up at the big rocket.

"There goes little Moonbeam," he said. "She's on her way!"

Soon no one could see the big rocket. It was too far up. But Scott went on looking after it for a long, long time.

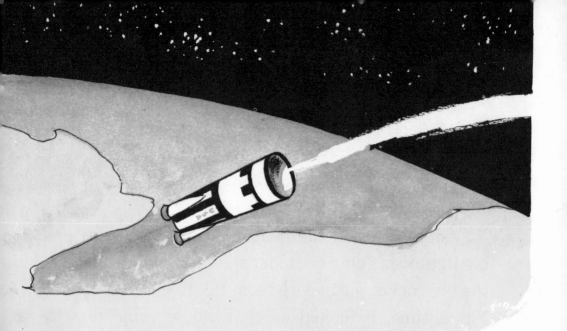

Laughing in Space

"Heeeeeeeen!" said Moonbeam.

She tried to get up, but she could not do it. In this part of the ride, right after lift-off, the rocket ship went faster and faster. For little Moonbeam, it was as if all of the big rocket was pushing down on her.

"Heeeeeeeeeeeeeen!" she said.

Little Moonbeam and the three astronauts were on their way to the moon at last. They were all happy about that. But this part of the ride was hard for little Moonbeam.

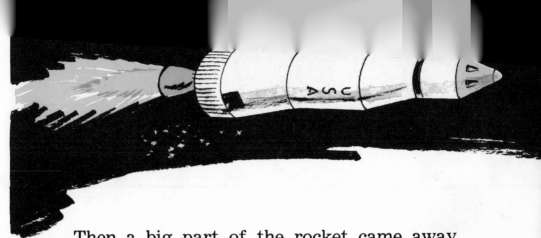

Then a big part of the rocket came away from the rocket ship. Soon the ship was going up very fast. It went as fast as it had to go. Now Moonbeam could lift her head. She could look at Dan Starr and the two other astronauts. Dan laughed.

"You will be all right now, Moonbeam," said Dan Starr.

"Hon, hon," said Moonbeam. "Hon, hon."

Moonbeam tried to jump. She wanted to play. She tried and tried to jump, but she could not get up. She was tied down. And she did not like it.

"Hon, hon, heeeeen!" she said.

"Now, now, Moonbeam," said Dan. "We will not let you jump around in the space ship. That would make trouble for all of us."

"Heen! Heen!" said Moonbeam.

Then Dan picked something out of his suit. It looked like a little ball.

"Look at this, Moonbeam," he said. "You will soon see what troubles we can have out here in space."

Dan lifted the ball up. Then he let it go. But the ball did not come down!

Moonbeam looked and looked. She did not know what to make of it.

"You see, Moonbeam?" said Dan Starr. "If you jumped up in space, you would not come back down again. Soon you would not know what is up, and what is down."

"You would not like it," said one of the other astronauts. "And you would be in Dan's way. Then he could not do his work right. The ship could be in trouble."

"Heeeeeeeen!" said Moonbeam. She put her head down. She had waited and waited for this trip. Now it was here, but she was not happy. She could not jump. She could not play. All she could do was be still and wait. . . and wait. . .and wait.

"Heeeeeeeen. . ." she said again.

Dan Starr had to laugh when he looked at her. But he did not like to see Moonbeam look so down. He wanted her to be happy.

"You will not have to wait long, Moonbeam," he said. "We will have to go out of the ship soon. There is work to do out there. And you can come with us."

Moonbeam looked at Dan. She just looked. The astronauts laughed.

"Moonbeam cannot know what you are telling her," said one of the men.

"She will soon see," said Dan.

The rocket ship went on and on.

Moonbeam looked at the men work. Then one of them said, "It is time."

"We have worked on the ship," said Dan. "We have it going right. Now we can go out of the ship."

"Hon?" said Moonbeam. "Hoon? Hon?"

Dan laughed. Then he opened the catch on a door. The door came open. And there, as far as they could look, was space!

"Come on, Moonbeam," said Dan. He opened a catch on Moonbeam's suit and picked her up.

Then, slowly, Dan and Moonbeam made their way out of the rocket ship. One of the other astronauts came out with them.

49

Dan let go of Moonbeam.

"You can look on from here, Moonbeam," he said. "But be a good chimp—no fast moves. If you want to play, you must move slowly."

The two men went to work.

"Do you see the little rocket ship tied on to our big ship?" Dan asked the other man.

"It is the ship we will ride down to the moon," said the man.

"Right," said Dan. "Our big ship can take us around the moon. But it cannot go down on the moon. This little ship will take us down. And it will take us back to the big ship."

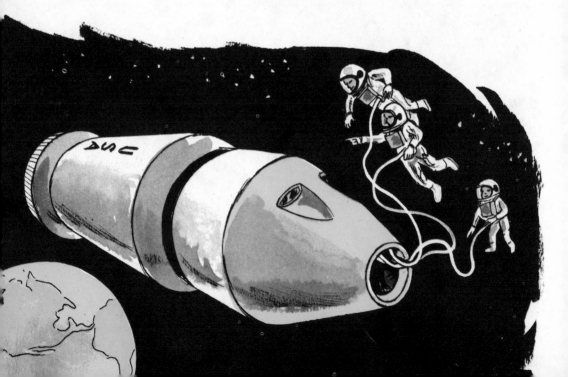

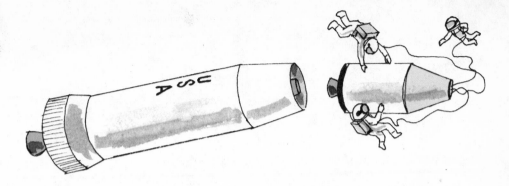

"Now we must turn the little ship around," Dan went on. "It must be turned the other way for the trip down to the moon."

The two astronauts went to work. They made no fast moves. Little by little, they moved the little ship away from the big ship.

It was slow going. The men looked at their work. They did not look at Moonbeam.

Slowly the little ship was turned around. When it was heading the other way, the men made it come back to the big ship. Then they tied it back on. The two ships were one again.

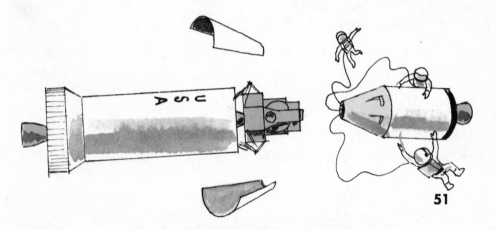

Part of the big rocket went with the little rocket. The other part would stay in space.

"But where is Moonbeam?" said Dan.

The men looked around, but they did not see the little chimp. Then—there she was!

Moonbeam was jumping and laughing! Out into space she would go! Then, back she would come! Jump! Laugh! Jump! Laugh!

"Moonbeam has space fever!" said Dan. The two men laughed and laughed.

UP went Moonbeam! DOWN she came!

Then Dan stopped laughing.

"You are moving too fast, Moonbeam!" he called out. "You will get hurt!"

Moonbeam went on jumping and laughing.

"Stop now!" called Dan.

Moonbeam did not stop.

"The space fever makes her do that," said Dan. "We will have to catch her and get her back into the ship."

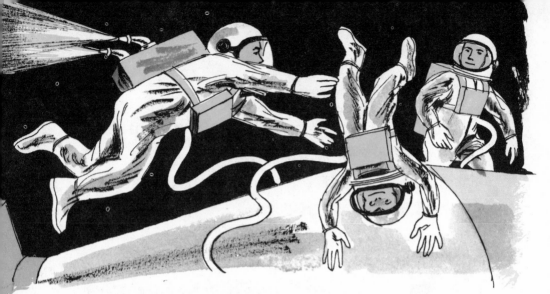

Slowly, the two men went after Moonbeam.
Dan came one way. The other man came the
other way. Moonbeam did not see them. She
did not see the ship. She did not see the moon.
She did not see space. All she could do was
jump this way, jump that way—this way—
that way.

"Now! Catch her!" Dan called out after one
of Moonbeam's jumps. "You can do it now!"

"I have her!" said the other astronaut.

Soon they had Moonbeam back in the ship.
Moonbeam looked at the three men.

"Hoon! Hoon! Hon, hoon?" she said.

"Her space fever has stopped," said Dan.
"And she looks happy now."

"What a funny chimp!" said the other men.

Down to the Moon

Two days came and went. The long rocket ride went on and on.

Part of the time, the men worked. At other times, Moonbeam and the men went to sleep.

When Moonbeam was not sleeping, she liked to look out into space. It looked as if the moon was getting bigger and
bigger and bigger.

"We are not far from it now," said Dan. "That is why it looks so big. Soon it will be time to go down on it."

"Hoon! Hoon!" said Moonbeam. She tried to jump up and down again.

"Now, now, Moonbeam," said Dan. "You will not have long to wait."

And it was so. The time soon came when Moonbeam looked out, and there was the moon, right under the ship! The moon's light was so white it hurt Moonbeam to look at it, and she had to turn her head away.

Then she turned back and looked and looked.

"Come on, Moonbeam!" came Dan's voice. Moonbeam turned to look at him.

"It's time," he said. "Time to go down to the moon!"

Dan and Moonbeam made their way slowly into the little rocket ship. Paul, one of the other astronauts, came too. The other astronaut looked at them from the big ship. He would wait there for them to get back.

In the little ship, Dan went to work. Slowly, he made the little ship take off. Little by little, it came away from the big ship.

"Here we go!" said Dan Starr.

Then Dan was still. So was Paul. This part of the trip would not take long, but the men had to look out for trouble all the way.

Down, down, down went the little rocket ship. Moonbeam looked out.

"Heeeeeeeen!" she said.

It looked as if the moon was coming up at them! They were going down fast.

"Heeeeeeeeeen!" Moonbeam said again.

Then Dan did something to the little ship. It jumped a little. It turned this way and that. Then, little by little, it slowed down. Soon it was moving very, very slowly.

And then it was still. They were on the moon now!

"We made it!" Dan called out.

"This is it—the moon!" Paul called out.

Dan Starr opened the door of the little ship. The two men and Moonbeam made their way down. Soon they were off the little ship. Two men and a chimp were on the moon!

The two men were so happy they did not know what to do. They jumped this way and that way, and around and around they turned. Moonbeam looked on. She did not know what to make of them. They looked like men, but they played just like chimps!

"Hon, hon! Hon, hon! Hon, hon!" said Moonbeam. She wanted to laugh and laugh. It looked as if the men had space fever now!

Soon Dan stopped jumping and turning.

"We will have time to play when we get back from the moon," Dan said. "Now we have work to do. Come on, you two!"

Moonbeam and the two men came away from the space ship. They went a little way. Then Dan turned to Paul.

"You go on this way," he said. "Moonbeam and I will go the other way. That way we will get to see a bigger part of the moon."

Moonbeam went with Dan. Moving on the moon was funny. Moonbeam could jump very, very far. She could not jump that far at home.

"Slowly now, Moonbeam," said Dan. "Being on the moon is like being very, very light. You take one jump and up and up you go."

As Dan moved on, he looked all around him. Back home, people would want to know what the moon is like. Now he tried to find a place in his head for all that he saw. "Then I can tell people what they want to know," he said. Dan worked and worked. He had no time to look after Moonbeam. Moonbeam would have to look after herself.

Trouble for Moonbeam

Moonbeam wanted to jump and play on the moon. But something in her head did not let her. She had work to do, too. She could still hear Dr. Jim's voice in her head. "Pick up a piece of the moon for me."

So Moonbeam went to work, too. She looked here and there. She would find a piece of the moon to take back to Dr. Jim. As Moonbeam looked, she moved on. Her head was down. She did not look at Dan. Dan worked with his head down, too. He did not see Moonbeam.

Little by little, Moonbeam moved away from Dan Starr!

Moonbeam looked and looked for a piece of moon for Dr. Jim. She came to a very big stone. She tried to lift it, and up it came!

"Hoon! Hoon!" said Moonbeam. Big stones were light on the moon. Lifting them was no work at all.

But this stone was too big for Moonbeam to take with her. It was too big to put in the little space ship. So Moonbeam put it down and moved on.

By now, Moonbeam had come far away from
Dan Starr. But she did not know that. She
looked on and on. She found stones that were
too big. She found stones that were too little.
But she did not find a stone that was just right.

"Heen, hon, hon, heen!" said Moonbeam.
What would she take back for Dr. Jim? She
was not happy at all.

Then Moonbeam did see something. She
looked again. There were the stones she was
looking for! She saw big stones, little stones,
long stones and other stones all together.
They were not far from Moonbeam.

To get to the stones, Moonbeam would have
to take a very big jump. If she did not make
it, down she would go, a long way down!

Moonbeam looked at the jump. Back home,
a jump like that would be too big for her. But
here on the moon, Moonbeam was light. Here
she could make it all right.

"Hon, hon, hon, hon," said Moonbeam. She
waited. Then she ran, and jumped. There was
no trouble. And there she was. All around her
were stones.

Moonbeam picked up stone after stone and looked at it. Soon she found the one she wanted. It was not too little and not too big. And it looked just like a little moon. Here was a piece of the moon for Dr. Jim!

Then the call came. It was Dan Starr's voice. "Moonbeam! Where are you, Moonbeam? It's time to get back to the ship!"

Moonbeam looked up. She did not see Dan. "Heen! Heen!" she said.

The little chimp moved fast. She picked up two other stones. She put all three stones in her space suit. Then she headed for the ship.

But Moonbeam was not looking where she was going! This time she did not look at the big jump she had to make. She did not wait. She wanted to get back fast. So she just made a jump.

It was not a good jump. For a time it looked as if she would make it. Then—back she went! And down she went!

She did not go far down. But she did hit her head on a big stone. Moonbeam was hurt.

"Moonbeam, it's time to head for home," came Dan's voice again. "Where are you?"

Moonbeam did not hear Dan's voice.

Moonbeam did not see where she was.

Moonbeam did not move at all.

Dan Starr was on his way back to the little spaceship. He had been too far away from Moonbeam to see her jump. Now he stopped and looked around. Soon Paul came up to him.

"What is it?" he said.

"That chimp must be playing and jumping around again," said Dan. "She will not come when I call."

"She may be in trouble," said Paul.

"And she may have space fever again," said Dan. "It would be just like her!"

Dan called Moonbeam again. So did Paul. Three times they called her. But Moonbeam did not come.

Dan looked at Paul.

"We don't have time to wait here for little Moonbeam," he said. "It will soon be time for the big spaceship to head for home."

"Then we must go and find the little chimp," said Paul.

So the two men went off to look for little Moonbeam. They could not see her.

The Chimp Lift

Dan and Paul looked and looked for little Moonbeam. They looked far and long. But they could not find her.

"Moonbeam must be in trouble," said Dan. "We would have found her by now if she was just playing."

The men went on looking. But time was running out.

"Soon we will have to stop looking," said Dan. "If we don't find Moonbeam soon, we will have to go home with no chimp."

The two men were not happy. They wanted to take Moonbeam back with them. They did not want her to stay on the moon.

"Moonbeam," Dan called again. "Where are you? Come to us."

Then Paul saw something.

"Look, there," he said to Dan. "Could our Moonbeam be down there?"

Dan looked.

"Come on," he said. "Let's find out!"

The two men moved fast now. Soon they came to a stop. And they looked down.

"There she is!" said Dan.

"What is she doing down there?" said Paul.

"I don't know," said Dan. He looked down at Moonbeam. "It's time to go, Moonbeam. Come on up," he called down.

The men waited. But Moonbeam did not move at all.

"Moonbeam!" called Dan. "Can you hear me, Moonbeam?"

Moonbeam could not hear him. She did not know the men were there.

"She must be hurt!" said Dan. "We must find a way to help her."

"But how will we get her up here?" Paul wanted to know. "If we don't do it fast, we will have to turn back. Then Moonbeam will have to stay down there."

"We will have to go after her," said Dan.

The two men worked and worked, but they could not do it. They could not get down to Moonbeam. She was too far down.

Then Dan looked at the time. He was not happy at what he saw.

"We cannot do it," he said. "We must get back to the little ship now. If we don't take off from the moon in time, we will not get to the rocket ship up there in space."

"But if we let Moonbeam stay on the moon," said Paul, "we will not see her again. No one will ever see the little chimp again!"

Dan Starr looked down again.

"I know," he said. "It cannot be helped."

Slowly, the two astronauts turned away. They wanted to stay. They wanted to help Moonbeam, but they could not do it.

Moonbeam would have to stay on the moon. No one would see her again.

Dan and Paul did not look back as they moved slowly away from Moonbeam. It was not a happy time. Then Dan stopped.

"Wait!" he said.

Paul stopped, too.

"What is it?" he said.

"I do have something that will help little Moonbeam!" said Dan. "Right here in my space suit!"

Soon he had it out. It was a long, long line.

"That could do it, all right!" said Paul. "We can get down to the chimp with that. But we must work fast!"

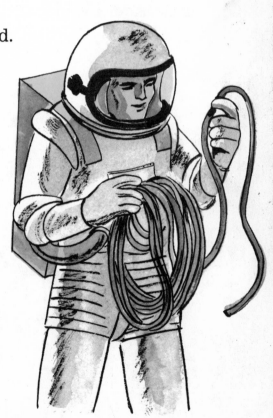

The two men went to work. They tied one part of the line around Dan. Then Paul let Dan down to where Moonbeam was.

Dan worked fast. He tied the line around Moonbeam, too. Then he picked Moonbeam up, and Paul went to work on the line. Soon he was lifting Dan and Moonbeam! He could lift them very fast. They were very light on the moon.

"Good work!" said Dan, when he and Moonbeam were back up with Paul. "We made it after all!"

But Moonbeam still did not move.

"She must have hit her head and hurt it when she went down," said Paul. "What can we do to help her?"

"We must get her back to the big spaceship fast," said Dan. "There we can take this space suit off her. Then we can have a good look at her."

"Let's go, then," said Paul.

He helped to tie Moonbeam to Dan's back. That way, Dan could see where he was going. And off they went.

Moonbeam Must Have Help

It did not take the two men long to get back to the little ship.

Again they tied the line around Moonbeam. Dan stayed down with Moonbeam. Paul went up into the ship with the line. From there he lifted Moonbeam. Dan helped with the lifting. Then he came up, too.

In the little ship, Dan looked at Moonbeam.

"She is still not moving," he said. "Tie her down, so she will not be hurt when we lift off. I will go to work on the little spaceship."

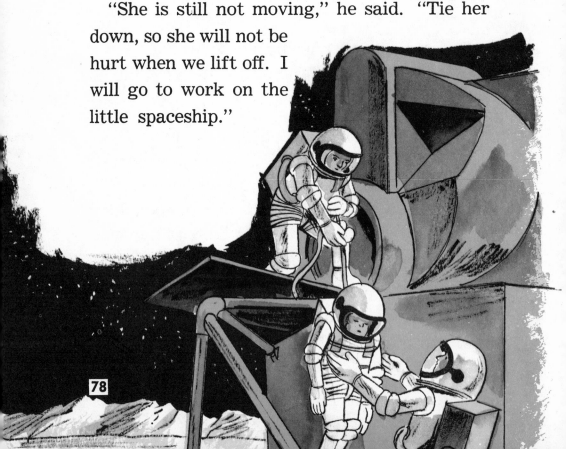

Dan worked on the ship. Paul worked on Moonbeam. Soon he had her tied down. Then Dan looked at the time. He called out.

"Three . . . two . . . one . , , LIFT-OFF!"

Slowly the little ship came up from the moon. Then, faster and faster it went. The two men looked out of the rocket ship. Under them, it looked as if the moon was coming away from the ship.

"No one has seen what we saw on this day," said Dan. "When we get home, people will want us to tell them what we saw and did."

"I know," said Paul. "And they will want to hear it again and again. It will take days and days!"

The two men laughed. Up from the moon and away came the little ship.

"We must be on the lookout for the big ship now," said Dan. "It will soon be time to tie up with it."

Paul looked out.

"There is it now!" he said.

"Where?" said Dan.

"Look, there!" said Paul. "See it?"

Dan looked and looked and looked. Then he saw something that looked very little.

"Now I see it!" he said. "It looks so little from here!"

But the rocket ship soon looked much bigger. Bigger and bigger it looked as they headed for it. Dan slowed down the little ship.

"Dan Starr calling! Dan Starr calling!" he said to the astronaut. "Can you hear me?"

"I hear you!" came the astronaut's voice from the big ship.

"Can you see us coming?" said Dan.

"I see you," said the voice. "You are heading just right!"

"Good!" said Dan. "Let's go to work, then! Let's put the two ships together!"

Dan opened the door of the little ship and the two astronauts made their way out. They went to work. Little by little, they moved the two ships together.

"A little to the right!" called Dan. "That's it! Tie that catch! Good! That will do it! We can get from one ship to the other now."

The two men went back into the little ship. Dan picked up Moonbeam. With Moonbeam, he and Paul made their way into the big ship.

The man in the big spaceship was happy to see his friends get back. But he was not happy to find out that Moonbeam was hurt.

"Can we help her?" he wanted to know.

"We will soon see," said Dan. "But now we must head this ship for home."

Dan Starr went to work. Catches came open. The two ships were not tied together now. Then the big ship moved away from the little ship. It was off for home.

The three astronauts looked back at the moon. It did not look very big to them now. Then they looked for the little ship. They could not see it.

"It will go on and on around the moon," said Dan. "We will not see it again."

Then Dan turned to Moonbeam. Soon he had part of her space suit off. He worked on her, but it did not help. He could not get her to move at all.

"I don't know what the trouble is," said Dan. "She has no fever. But I cannot make her come out of it."

"What can we do, then?" asked Paul.

"We must call home," said Dan. "They must have help waiting when we get back."

Dan called, "Moon ship calling! Moon ship calling! This is Dan Starr. Can you hear me? Can you hear me?"

The men waited.

Then a voice came from far away.

"We hear you, moon ship! We hear you, moon ship! Are you in trouble? Are you in trouble?"

"No trouble for us," Dan called back. "But Moonbeam is hurt. She must have help!"

Again the men waited. Again the voice came. "Help will be waiting!"

A Moon Stone for Dr. Jim

On and on the spaceship went. For two long days the ride went on. Time did not go fast for the three astronauts. They had little to do. And they were not happy to see Moonbeam so still.

"Come on, little Moonbeam," they said. "You can make it! You can come out of it!"

But Moonbeam did not see them. She did not hear them. And she did not move.

The men wanted Moonbeam to have help soon. They wanted to make the ship go faster, but it was going as fast as it could go. It was a long way from the moon back to the Rocket Port. They would just have to wait.

The two days went by slowly.

Soon it would be time for the big rocket ship to come down in the water on the earth.

Dan slowed the ship down. The astronauts could see the water now. It looked as if it was coming right up to their ship.

"Too fast!" said Paul to Dan.

Dan did something to the ship. Soon it was moving very slowly. Down, down, down it came. And then—WHUMP! SPLASH! It hit the water.

"That's it!" said the astronauts. "We are home again!"

It did not take long for other men to come. They went to work on the rocket ship. Soon it was lifted up out of the water. And after a fast ride, down it came on a big ship.

Dan picked up the chimp. Paul opened the door. And they all came out of the ship!

From all parts of the big ship happy men came running. General Winters was there, too.

"It is good to have you back from the moon,"
he said. "Your men can be very happy with
the good work that you did!"

The astronauts were happy with their good
work. But they were not happy that Moonbeam
was hurt.

"We must have help for Moonbeam right
now," said Dan.

"We have help for her," said General Winters.
Then he called out. "Dr. Jim! Scott!"

Scott and Dr. Jim came running up. Dan
Starr looked at Dr. Jim.

"Your head is still in white!" he said. "Why
did you come here?"

"My head will be all right soon," said Dr.
Jim. "But if Moonbeam had not helped me, I
would not be all right! Now I must see if I
can help her."

He went to work on the little chimp. He tried to help her in one way. He tried other ways. But they did not work. Moonbeam did not move. She did not come out of it.

"I can see what the trouble is with her head," said Dr. Jim. "But I cannot help her here. We must get her to the Rocket Port."

"Go fast, then," said General Winters. "We will soon come, too."

Dr. Jim, Moonbeam, and Scott were soon on their way. Up they came from the big ship. It was not a long trip.

"There it is!" said Scott. "The Rocket Port."

"We must come down there, where that house is," said Dr. Jim.

Down they came.

"Come on!" said Dr. Jim, as soon as they had come to a stop. Scott picked up Moonbeam. He and Dr. Jim ran into the house with her.

"Put her down here!" said Dr. Jim.

Dr. Jim went to work on her. He worked and worked. Moonbeam did not move.

Other people came one and two at a time. Dan Starr came. Paul and the other astronaut came. General Winters came. Jenny and Penny came, too!

They all wanted to know how Moonbeam was.
"Can you help her?" they asked Dr. Jim.

"I cannot tell now," said Dr. Jim. "But we will soon find out."

On and on he worked. The others waited. They were very, very still.

Then a little voice came.

"Honnnn," it said, and again, "Honnnn. . ."

"Moonbeam!" the call went up. "That was Moonbeam! Did you hear?"

Moonbeam was still for a time. And then Moonbeam moved!

She looked at Scott. She looked at Dr. Jim.
And she looked at all the others.

"Hon," she said. "Heen, hon, hon, hoon!"
The men all laughed.

"She is all right!" they said.

"Good work, Dr. Jim!" said General Winters.

Scott wanted to pick Moonbeam up. But the
little chimp was looking all around her. There
was something she wanted. Then she saw it.
It was her space suit.

Moonbeam ran to it. She looked and looked in it. And she found what she was looking for—the three stones that she had picked up on the moon!

Now Moonbeam ran back to Dr. Jim. The big stone was for him.

"You wanted a piece of the moon," said Scott. "Look! Moonbeam found one for you!"

Then Moonbeam ran to the girls. The two little stones were for them.

The girls were very happy.

"What a good friend you are!" said Jenny.

"All the people in town will want to see the moon stones!" said Penny.

"Hooooon! Hooooon!" said Moonbeam.

The men all laughed to see Moonbeam so very happy.

"It is good to have you back, little moon chimp!" they said.

VOCABULARY

The total vocabulary of this book is 187 words, excluding proper names and sound words. The 17 words in roman type should be familiar to children reading on a second-grade level. The 8 words above second-grade level are shown in italic type. The number indicates the page on which the word first appears.

astronaut 39	it's 23	*rocket* 5
bigger 55	*jeep* 7	ship 40
		slowly 8
chimp 5	lift 40	smiled 5
	lookout 15	*space* 5
		suit 36
faster 44	moon 5	
fever 5		tied 45
friendly 17	part 35	*tower* 15
	piece 38	trip 9
hit 13	push 43	trouble 12

J F M A M J J A S O N D — 7 1 7 0 6 9 6 8 6 7